VLAD

— AND —

TUTANKHAMUN'S TOMB

WRITTEN BY KATE CUNNINGHAM

ILLUSTRATED BY SAM CUNNINGHAM

Welcome, loyal subjects!

I am the mighty Vlad flea, and this is my friend Miu, slayer of snakes.

Usually we are supervising our chief servant Kel, and occasionally we allow him to sketch us to practise his skills as a tomb-painter.

It's hot work, but luckily we can cool off in the shade as we watch Kel work on a mural. Once we're sure he is doing it correctly we can have a little nap, so we have the energy to chase some rats later on.

Whilst we doze, our minds drift away from this valley, up the River Nile and back to the time of the old pharaohs. We imagine that we are modelling the body of an enormous cat, guarding the ancient pyramids over one thousand years before our current young pharaoh.

Three full moons ago, as we were floating through this favourite dream, it was rudely interrupted by voices crying and wailing. As they came closer we heard them screaming, "The pharaoh is dead. Tutankhamun is dead."

We sat up in shock. That can't be right. Tutankhamun is only nineteen years old.

The leader of the tomb-artists shouted for Kel.

"Hurry! There is much to do and we have only seventy days to complete the tomb. The gods will not wait for the paint to dry."

Miu followed Kel towards the ridge where the stonemasons have been hacking out the limestone to make Tutankhamun's chamber.

"No, no!" the foreman shouted as he chased us impatiently. "The plasterers are already working in the tomb of Ay, and as soon as they have finished, then the painting must begin."

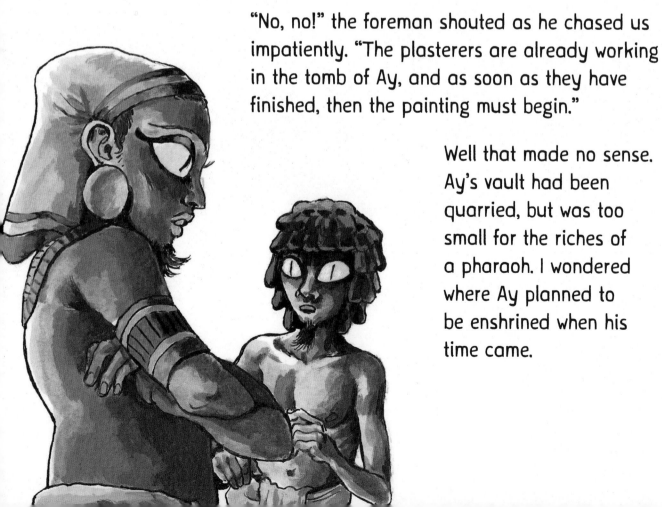

Well that made no sense. Ay's vault had been quarried, but was too small for the riches of a pharaoh. I wondered where Ay planned to be enshrined when his time came.

Outside the entrance a group of men were struggling to remove the wheels from chariots so they would fit through the narrow passageway. Servants were already carrying walking sticks and spears inside and piling them up in chaotic heaps.

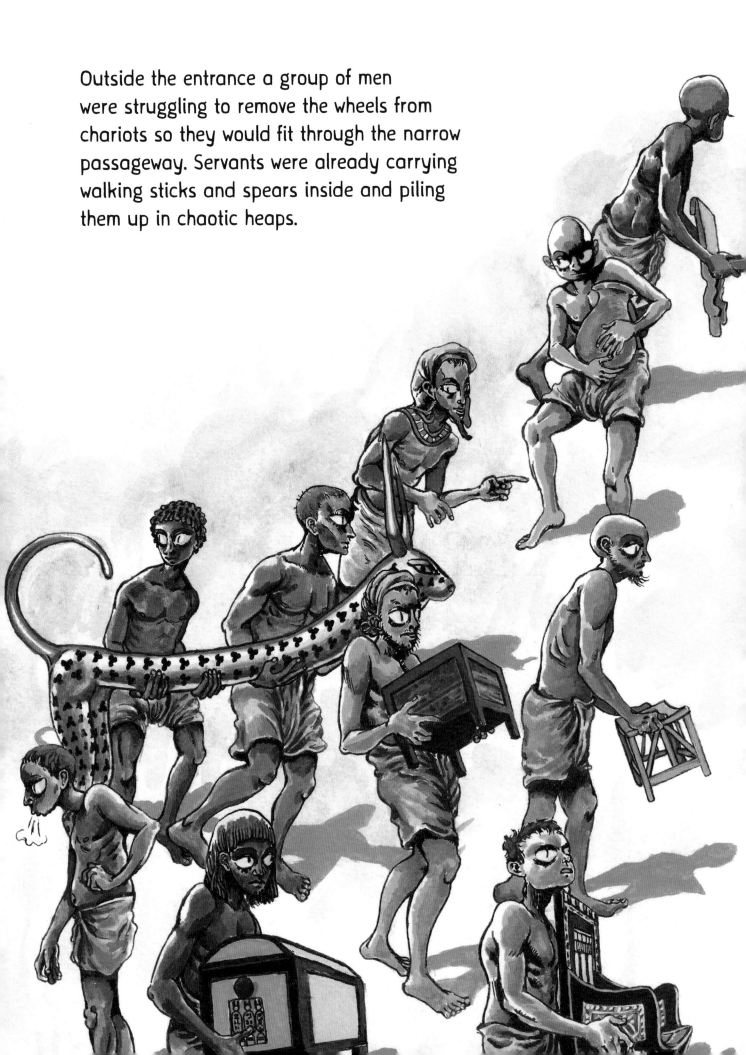

The smell of wet plaster was over-powering and Miu
was not impressed as she was kicked and jostled.
Nothing stands in the way of the burial of a pharaoh.

Kel joined the other painters ready to do his part. All around us people talked in shocked whispers, all trying to understand what could have happened to Tutankhamun.

"They say he fell from his chariot."

"They say it was the fever returned once more."

"They say he was assassinated."

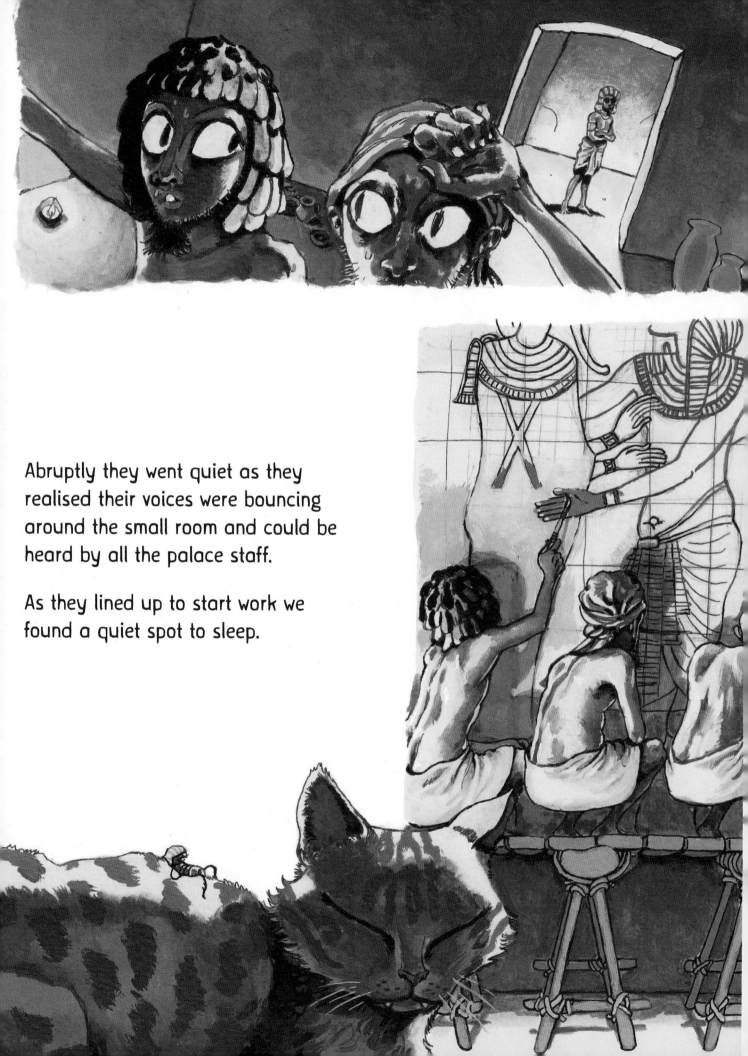

Abruptly they went quiet as they realised their voices were bouncing around the small room and could be heard by all the palace staff.

As they lined up to start work we found a quiet spot to sleep.

Hours passed and we lost track of whether it was day or night, or even how many times the sun had crossed the sky. Occasionally we came up the tunnel to the surface to get fresh air or hunt for food, and each time the rooms were more packed with gleaming statues, delicate shabtis and intricate treasure. Freshly cooked meats, bowls of nuts and jars of wheat were being prepared to feed Tutankhamun in the after-life. We lingered to sniff the wonderful smells, but it only made us more hungry.

Kel seemed to get no rest, but worked in a dazed frenzy; Tutankhamun's journey to the Field of Reeds had to begin on time.

As the men finally stepped away from their creation, Miu moved forward to gaze at it, mesmerised by the images and hieroglyphs on the wall.

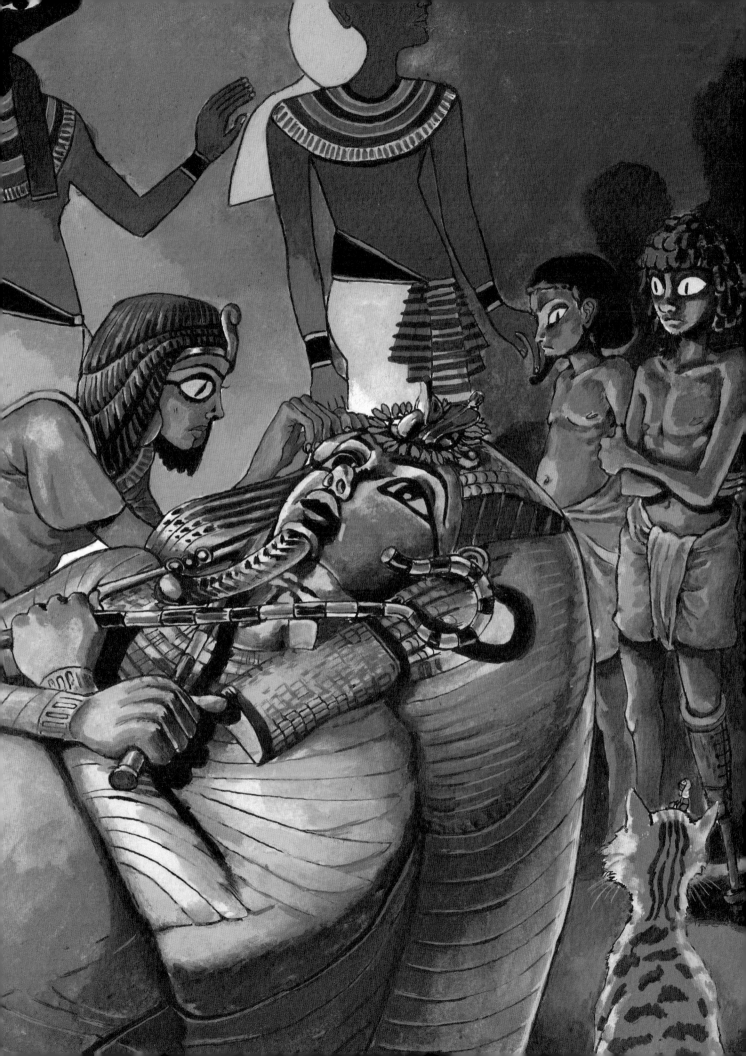

Suddenly I heard the scraping of stone against
stone and with a shock I realised what this meant.
They were sealing the tomb and we were still in it!

I tried a gentle tap to rouse Miu, but she was so engrossed she didn't notice. Now generally you are not meant to injure god-cats, but when you are in danger of being trapped for all eternity you need to take drastic action. Even deities feel a bite.

As we slipped through a small hole in the wall,
heavy rubble began to fall into the tunnel,
sealing it forever.

Miu and I were about to become permanent
features of this burial.

Finally she grasped the seriousness of the
situation and streaked between the raining
rocks. The darkness was closing in as we
raced to escape. Miu let out a huge yowl and
with a final effort lunged for the gap which
was lit only by the shards of light reflecting
off mountains of gold behind us.

Her head and body narrowly
slipped through the final gap . . .
but her tail did not.

We fled, and despite Kel's
calls, Miu ran to hide her pain
and embarrassment.

Eventually we returned to let Kel
nurse poor Miu, and he persuaded
a friend to make a replacement tail
of the finest materials.

Now I can tell my friend is dreaming
of the gleaming gold and our
close escape.

They say a pharaoh will live forever,
as long as people still say their name.

I wonder if they will remember Tutankhamun
three thousand years from now.

FACT FILE

- The ancient Egyptian civilisation lasted for over 3000 years (from 3100 BCE). This is split into three periods – the Old, Middle and New Kingdom.

- Tutankhamun became pharaoh at the age of 9, during the New Kingdom in the year 1336 BCE. The pharaohs had been ruling for 1700 years and the pyramids were already over 1000 years old.

- Miu is the first written name for a cat and reflects the sound they make. There are many images of wild and domesticated cats on tomb walls. Cats were also worshipped and linked to the god Bastet.

- The artists who worked for the pharaohs lived together in a village near the Valley of the Kings called Deir el Medina. It was excavated by Flinders Petrie who found many objects that tell us about the life of ordinary Egyptians.

- After Tutankhamun died, Ay became the next pharaoh and took the larger tomb for himself. However, it was a poor choice as Ay's tomb was robbed over the years, whilst Tutankhamun's lay almost undisturbed until it was discovered in 1922.

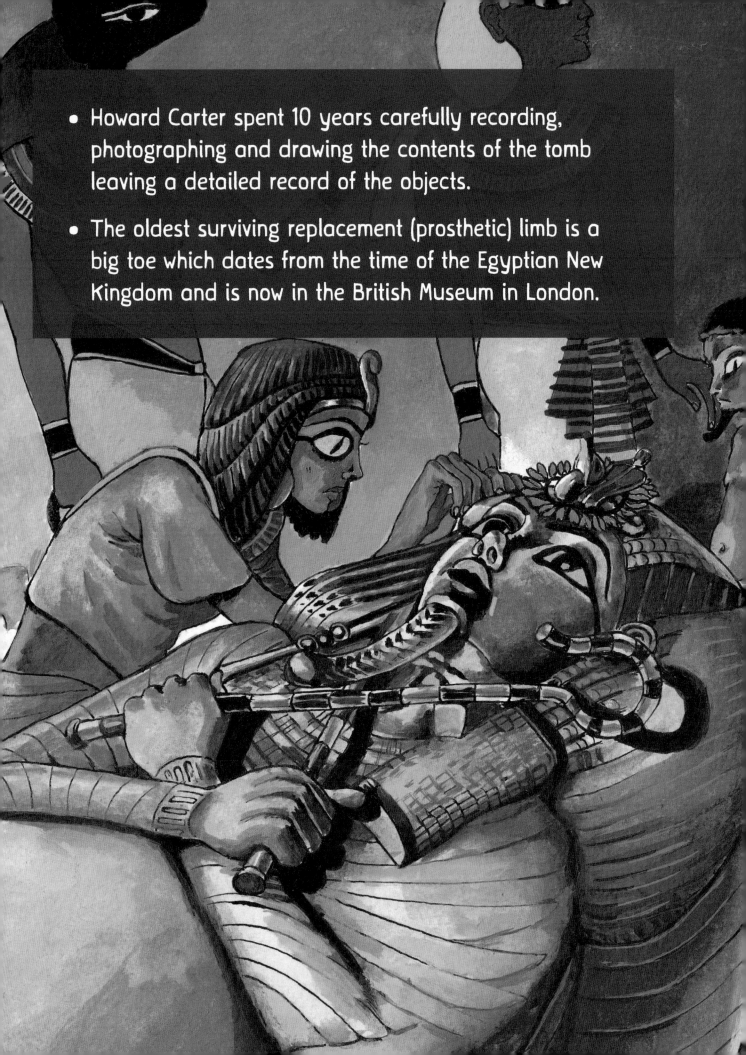

- Howard Carter spent 10 years carefully recording, photographing and drawing the contents of the tomb leaving a detailed record of the objects.

- The oldest surviving replacement (prosthetic) limb is a big toe which dates from the time of the Egyptian New Kingdom and is now in the British Museum in London.

This is how big Vlad really is

With thanks to the staff of the Petrie Museum for answering many strange questions.

Any errors are the responsibility of the author.

VLAD AND TUTANKHAMUN'S TOMB

Written by Kate Cunningham

Illustrated by Sam Cunningham

This paperback edition published 2020 by Reading Riddle

This edition designed by Rachel Lawston, lawstondesign.com

ISBN: 978-1-913338-03-9

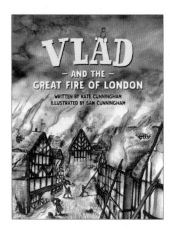
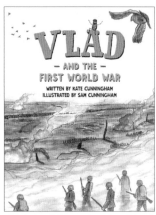

Printed in Great Britain
by Amazon

13021035R00020

VLAD
— AND —
TUTANKHAMUN'S TOMB

Tutankhamun has died suddenly and the rush is on to prepare his tomb. Vlad the flea and Miu the cat supervise the artists as they paint the murals. Will they finish in time, or will there be a sting in the tail?

ISBN 9781913338039

9 781913 338039

sweet dreams,

Moon
Baby

A Quilt to Make,
a Story to Read

Elly Sienkiewicz

5 Fanciful Heirlooms for Your Special Little One